savage

Originally published in French as *Sauvage* by Éditions Autrement, 2001

Library of Congress Cataloging-in-Publication Data

Jouet, Jacques.
 [Sauvage. English]
 Savage / by Jacques Jouet ; translated by Amber Shields. -- 1st English
translation.
    p. cm.
 ISBN 978-1-56478-535-0 (pbk. : alk. paper)
 1. Gauguin, Paul, 1848-1903--Fiction. 2. Painters--France--Fiction. I.
Shields, Amber. II. Title.
 PQ2670.O926S2813 2009
 843'.914--dc22
                              2008050088

Partially funded by a grant from the Illinois Arts Council, a state agency, and
by the University of Illinois at Urbana-Champaign

Ouvrage publié avec le concours du Ministère français chargé de la culture
– Centre national du livre.

This work has been published, in part, thanks to the French Ministry of
Culture – National Book Center.

www.dalkeyarchive.com

Cover: design by Danielle Dutton, art by Nicholas Motte
Printed on permanent/durable acid-free paper and bound in the United
States of America

savage

by Jacques Jouet

Translated by Amber Shields

Dalkey Archive Press
Champaign and London

The pages presented here with the curt but comprehensive title of *Savage,* as well as an indication of their genre (novel), were not found, half mutilated, in the false bottom of a secret drawer, or in a privateer's chest, hidden in the attic of some manor. The material in them wasn't gleaned from the lips of a dying man anxious for his tale to enter an attentive ear. They weren't rescued from the temporary obscurity to which I don't know how many of my servile creatures—characters, despite themselves, in the following story, and pseudo-occupiers of its alleged appendices— might have wished to banish them.

These pages are rightfully mine, as far as they can be possessed, and there is no reason to delay my clear identification of myself as the author, once and for all—that is, simply to refer the reader back to the words on the cover of the work being held in her eager, if still hesitant, hands.

We exchange words of welcome . . . *enchanté* . . . pleased to meet you . . . We understand each other this way, and everyone plays his own uninterchangeable role. If my name is on the cover, the *ex libris*, on the inside, bears the name of the reader. I won't reveal this name—with a little luck, there may be several. Yes, let's tell each other these pleasant things, before the hostilities begin.

In this age, when historical research has been carried to such a pitch, it wasn't my lot to discover—almost miraculously—a manuscript still completely unknown. Nobody came to ring my doorbell or rap at my window, no peculiar individuals with eight-day beards, holding bundles of papers under their arms—bequeathed to them by some friendly hand under circumstances worthy of a novel. No, fortune didn't drop an elderly doctor in my lap, in possession of a lead case, which he'd claim to have unearthed in the foundations of an ancient hermitage during its restoration. It's quite unlikely that these pages were found at a rummage sale of manuscripts and old papers, since I conceived of them myself. It's even less likely that I uncovered them in a cottage in a rather remote corner of the kingdom of Aragon, since I mulled over them for a long time, cast them as fastidiously as one would cement, happily covering them with ink, and always fine-tuning them. No, I didn't dig up these pages in an unused soup kettle, a bathtub-turned-storage-locker, or in the back corner of some musty shed; nor did I find them in a hat, on the banks of the grassy waters of the Marne, on January 11, 1904. I did not want to insert my own words, thus impairing the somewhat corrosive grace of the so-called journal of some chambermaid. I did not have to ask, as recompense for my pains, permission to cut anything which, in my opinion, might not be to the purpose. I did not wait, rooted to the ground, for a mysterious correspondent to send documents to me, enjoining me to prepare henceforth a typescript in accordance with the guidelines for publication, but without allowing anything to be printed before a strict delay was observed. No, these lines were not found among the papers of some traveler in Central Europe, North Africa, or the Far East, who is reputed to have settled in Bouville three years ago to conclude his historical research on the Marquis de Rollebon.

In light of this fact, which I now believe to be well established, I will not hide behind the fallacious label of "Editor." I will seek out a different model for that indispensable precaution, the initial formula of fiction—carrying, inside, its seed of doubt, hopefully delicious, as well as its poison. And if there's poison, I'd like to rid it of any trace of bitterness.

This novel being a work of fiction, and this work of fiction being a novel, it would hardly be absurd to assume that the author ought to be held accountable for the consequences of any potential, apparent resemblances in his text to places, exclamations, words, gesticulations, or people belonging not to his story but, accidentally, to reality. Shall we all agree here and now that the orchard of coincidence won't produce any of its infamous fruits this year? If such a contract ordinarily goes without saying, giving it voice here will hardly make it any less binding. In case of any dissatisfaction, please direct all complaints to the author, rather than his characters, which latter have no more claim to the title of saint than the former has to that of an "almighty" God.

These few prefatory lines, which—like those that follow—were by no means dug up in Ile de France at the foot of an old clock tower, in a little house, in a locked attic, in the secret compartment of a trunk where they had been deposited by a Spanish prisoner . . . These lines, which are not from a manuscript written in Newgate Prison and dropped by chance into my hands, to be polished and perfected, by a fleeing madman . . . These lines, I say, are no longer prefatory lines or pages. There's no reason to believe they were written in 1827. They weren't drafted by a certain Captain Georges, who would have liked for one of his crewmen to read them. These pages are neither discolored nor effaced, they haven't been mutilated in any way, aren't preceded by the words "preface," "foreword," or "note to the reader"; not even by the word "prologue," which I did consider momentarily. They won't be interrupted by any interludes, because each one, except the first and the last, already serves as an interlude between two others. They are all already part of the murky disarray that will, necessarily, add another little burden—that of having to synthesize things seen with things imagined—to the shoulders of their readers, most of whom don't give a good goddamn about them. And if these words are meant to hold their clients' attention, if they've been even slightly successful up to this point, it would hardly be prudent to waste this advantage by inserting a big blank space, or even a page break—or a "Chapter Two," never having been announced by a "Chapter One"—instead of entering into my narrative without any further ado: thus, *in medias res*, at a point in this story that's neither at the beginning nor the end, and not a random occurrence but an intentional act, taking place behind a certain individual's brow, as well as beneath his pen, tracing first the word *This*, then the word *is,* then the two words *my last,* followed by still others, making up: *This is my last will and testament, revoking all prior wills and codicils . . .* It bequeaths nothing of any value to anyone, but is a simple testimonial—duly authorized and, perhaps, final.

No, the civilization that had cultivated Paul, the civilization that had cultivated me, me, no longer held me dear—it hadn't for quite a while, and didn't care about what I meant to offer it in return.

I was, however, civilized, and my ancestors as well, from Paul to Paul, since the very beginning of all the centuries my memory had accumulated. I folded my lettuce without tearing the leaf and peeled my pear with a fork and a knife.

Too young, I had started out in finance, at the very bottom of the ladder and, never having found a reason to explore the higher rungs, I remained a little account-book rat with his incisors in the flesh of his bread.

I was a man still in a formative state.

When the time came, I served my country in the navy, mostly working with machines in the lower decks when, earlier, I had dreamed of being up in the crow's nest. I was honest with my superiors, courteous with my peers. There was never anyone under my own command.

For a long time, from the day I first had to earn a living—an obligation forced upon me too early by the death of my parents—I never stopped chasing after every three sous, and soon I had one, then two, then three, then four, then five, then six children to share them with. Six kids, and more than enough. Each of them had the appetite of twelve and each was bigger than the last, growing exponentially.

Pauline, my wife, didn't waste any time in declaring me a lost cause, deciding I'd wronged her and that I hadn't been there for her when she needed me. She never went back on this judgment. May her still-living (I imagine) body rest in peace. And may her embittered spirit rest in peace as well.

My case was calamitous, yes, but not right from the beginning.

I was born in a passably favorable region, an Anjou halfway between city and country, where a fire in a factory would result in the rehiring of its workers in order to rebuild it. The owner would tighten his belt a little and, two or three years later, prosperity would return. At least that's what was said publicly; it was a gross overgeneralization. It was a harsh world, but not lacking in courage and civic-mindedness—qualities I was determined to lose, since it's a known fact that the people who are usually the first to benefit from them are the same ones who consider their absence a virtue.

My father was a clerk in the civil service and played the horses.

Severe and unyielding, my mother had, very distantly, the blood of certain South American tropical countries in her veins, a fact that she kept hidden, as though it was a terrible disgrace. Of course she wasn't as severe as all that. I never once succeeded in getting her to talk about her early childhood, nor speak in the language she probably spoke as a child. I am able to deduce with some certainty that Spanish was her first language, but I never knew for sure. I was never allowed to probe further. It didn't matter to my father that she wasn't an Anjou native, but nonetheless, he never revealed her deception when she shamelessly indulged in it, saying she was born in Feneu and raised in Ponts de Cé.

My father died of pneumonia after a trip into the wine cellar. His wife, my mother, though she was a more moderate drinker, followed in his footsteps, faithful to the last.

As far as money went, my inheritance was a trench of debt. I hadn't expected it would be quite so bad. In the presence of the notary, there was nothing I could do but sign away what little had been left to me—something that can't be done without at least a symbolic sense of bitterness. I read ferocity in the notary's words and contempt in his handshake.

I had no brothers or sisters. I became free and without estate.

After a few years of purely vegetative survival in a hovel paid for by the civil service, I finally pulled myself together with a violence born of conviction—even if this conviction was founded on a gaping question rather than a solid answer. If I abandoned the lower ranks of a mediocre career in finance with excessive haste, it was only because I had some new ideas and perspectives in the works.

"What, at this point in time, can we make of a man?"[†] That was the question I continually asked my friends and myself. Every moment in the world is always accepted by the masses as a relatively definitive fact. Man as a species is at an impasse. Whether this or that individual is comfortable (I won't even say "happy") in light of these circumstances is another affair, clearly more nebulous. There are only a few learned people who might think the world might be otherwise, a few doctors not resigned to this or that decrepitude, a few revolutionaries, like my great-aunt Flora Tristan, who didn't have Isolde's beauty, even though I wished it for her.

I learned to speak the French of France and the Loire Valley, and to write testamentary French, so belabored and placid it could make death itself sound unimportant (isn't it, after all, a fairly common occurrence?)—otherwise, my testament would be written in pidgin French, a language that I also conquered, as the reader will see, if the coursing of my blood, the pump (and pomp) that drives it, give me enough time to tell all.

What, at this point in time, can we make of a man?

I repeat this question, which I've asked myself many times—not only yesterday, but often, on my way to Peru and back by boat; and there among the miners, in my shiny office, smelling of ink and old paper; and among my children, from whom my only thought was to flee toward endless barroom arguments—verbal jousts that take place far from children and virtuous women.

What, now, can *I* make of a man, in the time allotted for the feat assigned to me?

It could be a poet's question, or the question of a novel-ist, full of ambition and unfinished chapters, or a dramatist capable of writing a five-act play. Literature was a domain I considered more within my reach than science or de-utopified socialism. My attempts were disastrous. I left *The Urban Adventures of Sebastien Froissart* unfinished, which—had I had the tenacity to lay out the consequences of my first axioms and get beyond the inevitable reactions of the bourgeoisie—would have amply addressed the tendentious subject of a workers' republic. But I lacked the courage to really destroy a world after having built a new one. It didn't stand up. I changed tone on immersing myself in the battle of the social classes, not really knowing to which I belonged. I dashed off a pitiful yet edifying tale in the Hugolian manner of *Poor Folk*, which was quickly trumped by Baudelaire's reading in *"Assommons les Pauvres!"* And to top it all off, I purely and simply gave up on a play I'd been writing that was meant to be performed in installments—a kind of theatrical equivalent to the step-by-step gait of a newspaper serial—which I had entitled *The Nouvist Man*: a different act would be turned in every evening for the ac-tors of the Boulevard Saint-Martin, ten minutes of theater that would be added on to the preceding acts and grow like an infinite rosary. I lost myself in the *Nouvist* caravan and soon my ten fingers ceased production, stopped any sort of written invention, and quietly returned to their shoddily patched pockets.

It is in this context that my trip to Peru took place; it was stupidly undertaken because of the ramblings—as unverified as unverifiable—of a mining engineer, also from Anjou, who was dreaming of a certain yellow metal. Six months of wandering and fevers ended with the burial of my engineer, dead along with his entire family, having caught a fever even yellower than his dream. I wasn't cut out to be a miner, even under the open sky, even of gold.

And even supposing I went to the Americas in search of my mother's roots (which I acknowledged only with repugnance), it was a great deal of trouble for nothing. I ended up deciding it was more likely that she was only from Extremadura or Galicia. I stopped thinking about it.

One day, later, when I was visiting a very formal art exhibition in Paris, brimming with new ideas and notably with the anticipation of my own possible success in the world of painting, I heard the distinct voice of a visitor who stood out from the crowd due to his peremptory and unrestrained conviction. Parked in front of a full-length portrait of a certain baron of industry or finance, today as perfectly forgotten as his portraitist, the speaker was saying, more or less, that, indeed, the frock coat in the painting was skillfully rendered, but that someone contemplating it couldn't imagine that the painting's model had had any lungs. He continued his scathing commentary in the same vein. This man who was speaking so clearly was a certain Édouard Manet; a relatively obscure name. His words had an unexpected effect on me. I owe the biggest decision of my life to him. He said, exactly:

"I can see that someone has painted a frock coat. Everything leads me to believe it is a frock coat. This frock coat itself is of an impeccable cut. But where are the model's lungs? He isn't breathing under his garment. He has no body. It's a portrait for a tailor."

Don't think that this revelation of a true painter's formidable eye turned me once and for all to the profession in which he himself probably excelled (it wasn't long before I was sure that this "probably" was superfluous). It was in completely different terrain that I had the idea of planting my little pieces of wood, in hopes of their regaining their vigor like the scrawny trees in the Antilles that always end up yielding apples and papayas—at least according to the colonialists.

The question I've already mentioned wouldn't stop bothering me; it was even worse once I thought I'd caught a glimpse of the beginnings of an answer.

What one can make of a man at this time is his body.

Not his body as box of suffering, not his body as aging mass, and not even his body as sack of delight or admirable mass of muscle. I should really explain what I mean. But first, to this end, I'll have to describe another encounter.

Although my displacement in Peru had, as I said, not been beneficial in the least, I was at least remunerated for my wanderings upon my return by my acquaintance with an eccentric old lady, for whom I must say a few words of eulogy. Madame Taillefeu-Ponçard wore her eighty years well. She would say, "Eighty winters and not eighty springs, because winter preserves things better." As little as she resembled Édouard Manet, she shared his taste for an exercise that she formulated thus:

"There's nothing I hate more than a passive glance."

She was circumspect, generous, and implacable. She felt that her advanced age obliged her not to give people advice, but to teach each person something, and preferably something pertinent to that particular individual. This day, by the way, it was my turn. My lesson was delivered on a passenger liner on the ocean, off the Azores—whose whaler's huts, with a little imagination, we could almost see on the horizon. Smiling, slightly mocking, Madame Taillefeu-Ponçard eyed me from head to foot, continuing, in an alternately hesitant and determined voice:

"So my dear, admit that you yourself . . . you'll let me call you Paul . . . forgive me if I embarrass you . . . you shouldn't hide your muscles. I saw you yesterday, on the gangway. I got a better look at you this morning. Believe me, people don't know how to coordinate their clothes with their naked bodies. I say this with all due respect."

These words, a rare truth, struck my ears, fitting into them like a perfectly formed tenon fits into its mortise in a wooden construction—built to last—or like a button in a buttonhole. The reader can choose the image that suits him best.

I was on the second-class deck when she addressed me from up above, leaning her elbows on the first-class guardrail. She generously invited me to join her by effecting an athletic ascent over the barrier, and to chat with her about passersby, which was her specialty. And I accepted.

"If looking at something-or-other bothers you, look closer," she said. "That's my philosophy. For example, my little Paul, look over there at the Columbian ambassador and his wife. The fact that they are (miraculously) recovering from malaria is no excuse for their almost indecent clothing—I mean, indecent above all for themselves, besides being indecent for each other, besides, again, being indecent for those of us who have to look at them, since they parade in front of our eyes without the least bit of shame. They represent the French Republic—the proudest Republic in the world . . . proud, in fact, to the point of wanting to engulf that world entirely—" (I'm not arguing, for the moment, whether she was right or wrong; we'll come back to that later, if you like) "—and they do so with their bodies stuffed into those tarps as though they were vulgar, unpresentable machines, when today even locomotives are so beautifully displayed . . . He doesn't have enough of a neck already, he needs a high collar to double it! The gentleman's Adam's apple should be restrained! And Madame's clavicles, overly thin and jutting out like a ship's prow, shouldn't have to sustain the sea spray's assault. It's ridiculous. All dressed up like a chauffeur, or a deep-sea diver, or covered in mosquito netting . . . They're dressed like they're going skiing in Chamonix . . . Protection, protection . . . Their clothes are so tight at the ankles and wrists that they look like they're getting ready to go tarantula hunting. Or these veils, for when you're collecting honey . . . Women wear them, can you believe it, just to go do a quarter of an hour's shopping at La Ferté-sous-Jouarre, bargaining with the suntanned peasant women, their cheeks exposed, wearing folded newspapers as hats! Apparently this protects them from the flying fish . . . bang! right in their eyes, fragile as eggshells. And what do you think of those superfluous horn buttons, which neither attach to nor close anything? Isn't their principal effect to bury the navel or the billiard-balls of their eyes in a drove of false look-alikes? Nothing is where it belongs anymore. That man looks like his wife and that woman resembles her poor husband. But they no longer resemble human beings: they've been redesigned. And it's not just because their faces are powdered that they're fair game. See those military men over there? Tell me if they don't look like battlefield priests with their bronze collars and tiepins, or combat Franciscans, even though Franciscans have the elegance to go barefoot? It's just not possible . . . our officers tailor their clothing with wire cutters! They must think they're putting on copper sheaths, or zinc roofing! They must get undressed with a monkey wrench! The captain? There he is, white and navy blue all over! Is the ocean always white and navy blue? He's wearing so many stripes that he looks dressed up like a pork roast. Can you see the air moving? Watch his sleeves! His second mate is only a little roast piglet, dreaming of getting fattened up, while the stewards are forever in celluloid. Do you know the story of the Italian immigrant who, out of respect for his new country, dons his smoking jacket as soon as he catches sight, from the boat, of the port of New York, but who, then, out of despair, throws himself into the bay (he can't swim) when he sees the NO SMOKING sign . . . As for that woman there, I'd ask, 'what became of her breasts?' if I weren't so disinclined to alliterate. I'm not saying she should frame them like a Botticelli, but passersby should at least be able to imagine where they might be. As she is now, they're simply not there. The lady has uprooted them. And let's not even talk about the children . . . or yes, let's: they're clowns. Or, quiet now, they're dwarves. It's better if they don't hear us. I only hope that little boy holds onto some of the perverseness that leads him to play by himself in his mother's closet . . . I sense that you're seeing me through different eyes now . . . and you're surely thinking that I don't practice what I preach."

"Not at all, you're quite elegant!"

I wasn't flattering her.

"If you say so! But I'm a very old lady and what I want to teach you is only a theoretical science. If I were you, I'd throw myself into the water—metaphorically speaking, of course. I'm not forgetting we're at sea. Ding-dong. That's the dinner bell. Dine with me this evening and we'll talk of other things, yes? We can as easily make much the same observations about cooking, or music, or gardens . . . or poetry."

That evening, however, Madame Taillefeu-Ponçard and I did not talk of other things, since the available targets had all changed their clothes for dinner. There was even a faint smell of soap and shampoo. By way of a practical exercise, she asked me to take a turn at critiquing, one by one, the regulars at the dining room, the majority of which had made a pathetic effort to dress solemnly.

I didn't have Madame Taillefeu-Ponçard's nerve, but she had already given me a little bit of her eye—just enough to open mine. I tried not to let anything escape me. There was a lot to be said, and I strove to say it all. She was pleased with me. I permitted her to conclude:

"You're on the right track. They dress up simply because it passes the time, gives the help something to do, and naturally they can't not have servants if they want to maintain their status. But where is the creativity?"

There wasn't even a fraction of an ounce.

I related to Madame Taillefeu-Ponçard what Édouard Manet had said about the lungs in the frock coat. Her eyes shone. She said I was on fire, that that was exactly it. But real-life frock coats should also have lungs. It was necessary to start there. It was up to me to start there. She added that I already had the inclination.

At the last onboard party, there was an accident. The train of a dress got caught in the crank of a mechanical piano, only to reveal a body that then courageously hid its curves behind the billiard table in the ballroom. This was quite a beautiful moment of artistic discretion that gave me a little more encouragement (if any were needed) to follow the path mapped out for my future.

When the passenger liner docked at Le Havre, I had honed my criticism to the point of feeling ready to draw up my first models. However, I first wasted six months floundering in the industry's pusillanimous myopia. I was under the illusion that I could break into the profession without first suffering humiliation at the hands of the conventions that were then in place. A few bold colors, a few slightly exaggerated gaps in the fabric, and a few long days didn't constitute a style. They only testified to the clumsiness of a mildly conceited careerist who hadn't gone to the right schools and didn't even know there were right schools to go to.

So I took to walking in the streets, thinking, with my hands always deep in my pockets, but my head never in the clouds.

If I wanted to make something of the body of man, obviously I had to start by undressing him, by contemplating the model itself, just as the ancient painters who always sketched their subjects nude before painting their clothing had done. All the unfinished Davids had something to teach whoever wanted to look at them.

I hired models, whom I stood in front of me, nude. An enormous coachman, who had posed as the model for a Balzac character, and drew from this a Balzacian hauteur; a beautiful laundress who felt rather self-conscious; a very slender dancer. I ruined myself to pay them particularly well, since there was one small condition to our transaction: it was of principal importance that I be just as naked as they were, during the posing session: this in the name of putting myself in their skin, putting myself inside the nakedness of my models, albeit—let no one misunderstand me—in complete chastity. I considered my nudity a rule of decorum, whose function was not to facilitate intimate relations between myself and my models, but, if the occasion arose, and the desire manifested itself, to confine them to the realm of the imagination.

I studied. I drew. I shaped. The coachman was the site of a beautiful clash between fat and muscle, with thickset bones, heavy as cast iron, acting as arbitrators. The laundress had the whiteness of a diaphanous silk sheet that was lovely to look at, but a color with which any piece of clothing would have to do battle with. The dancer had burnished brown skin good enough to lick. My cheek a few centimeters from her body, I could gauge the heat that emanated from her. Bread in a toaster.

In order to broaden the scope of my understanding, I also worked on a young woman who was not so beautiful. And a decrepit old man. I had to utilize a great deal of effort not to see this as some sort of punishment. I utilized it.

As for myself, I completely renovated my wardrobe, plunging into designing a style of ample and malleable ease, groping all the while for a suitable artistic precision: figuring out how the comfortable could also be beautiful. Never wear anything while alone that wouldn't work just as well in company. Clothing: a second skin, more intimate than the first because it was chosen specifically in a shop in order to be seen in public. And a skin that changes. The body changes attitude when it changes attire.

I began to go out in the street more or less naked, barelegged for example, my shirttails hanging down to my thighs, but with a quite distinguished upper body. People didn't like it much. The neighbors never got used to it.

Without a word to my wife I had rented a workshop far from my little family, who I hardly even thought about feeding anymore. It was at this point that Pauline removed herself from me for good, and removed me from our children. Wanting to deprive me of all of them, the woman who'd renounced me found it both urgent and reasonable to expatriate herself, or rather to repatriate herself, with all our children, to Copenhagen, her place of birth. It was a transitional solution I didn't much approve of, though it suited me well enough. She was leaving me enough elbow room to succeed in starving to death all by myself, or else, at some time in the future—if fortune were to smile on me—to become the head of a family finally basking in all the wealth that I'd never known: the head-of-family that I'd never been. (And, I can add today, at race's end: that I will never be.)

After their departure, I missed one child in particular, my favorite, whom I had watched most closely during the spectacle of their childhood: Claire, who seemed extremely mature on some days—ripe like a woman of thirty-five years (a bourgeois city woman)—and whose mother often accused her of lewdness. Certain gestures, it's true, that the other children would only have risked in a fit of fever came naturally to her—tearing clothes, ripping them off, or throwing themselves, in the summer, into an inviting stream. It was she who would come to tell me good-night completely naked, her true naughty little girl's slit on display, arms and legs stretched to form an X. She died too young, still small, and far away from me, trying to tear off her poisoned skin, which itched excruciatingly. I was told that in her delirium, she wanted me to come and pick up her sickness, to throw it in the garbage the same way I used to clean up the room she shared with her brothers and sisters, sparing no scrap of litter. She cursed me for not coming. But it's of her, nonetheless, that I think, while drafting these testamentary lines—she who will never read them.

Becoming a body-smith requires a much greater asceticism than people think. Everyday requirements suddenly fade into the background, and one only wants to speed through the stages of one's work . . . which is, however, no easy task.

And sexual relations slow everything down.

Bar tabs, debts, and unpaid loans are all without interest. The only things that matter are the passionate, interminable discussions between friends from all levels of prosperity, including the failures you happen to be close to and who have something to teach you despite their misfortune.

I felt like I was flying. I was enthralled by the complexity of my objective, the body, the meeting place of matter, heat, and color, with the miracles of its joints, its machine-like propulsion . . .

Then came a period of complete liberty, of active bohemianism, that today I look back on as a time of great happiness—but one mustn't trust the affective memory, which easily erases all the discouragement and lethargy of the transitory moments between two peaks.

I wanted Manet to be convinced of the flagrant injustices perpetrated on the tailor, and that clothing design should be placed as high as the work of Delacroix and Rubens. I turned up my nose at the preordained hierarchy of the arts that only served to put soapbox intellectuals—craning their necks like arrogant giraffes—on a pedestal.

It was then that I decided to change methods, beginning by adopting an entirely new one. I took a backwards approach to clothing, turning it inside out as one skins a rabbit, trying to escape all convention.

I got myself out of my impasse by dint of analysis.

I espoused the pleasure of rational displacement and antonymy. Some examples follow.

I tried to imagine what underpants for the head would look like. Socks for the hands. An anal hat. Outer underwear ... and a base for this outer underwear: an overcoat of skin, like a furred nightgown. Then a buttocks-bra, a sexhibition, a stomach-collar, and ear-shoes. A skirt for the torso, or a neck-warmer. Breastlace, asslace (which I thought I had invented, but which I later discovered already existed in darkest Africa). I designed the thigh vest and the pelvis sleeve. The bicep garter. The arm-trouser. A muff for the waist ... which makes a woman into a flexible tube—she gives birth to herself when she undresses.

I sketched. I cut, I stitched. I assembled materials and colors. I fashioned buckles, straps, knots. I tested adhesives, all sorts of adhesives, with little success. At the time, these fittings were still secret. I dreamed of a public presentation.

I had a severe and contradictory debate with Louis Sébastien, the meritorious composer of "Skies Over Mt. Ventoux," of "Paris from My Sole" (the shortest piano piece in the repertoire), as well as of that strange comic opera in which the principal singing role is Ulysses's old dog, containing a duet where the returning hero imitates his old quadruped companion's bark in order to identify himself. Yes, Louis Sébastien, who never found success, but never lost his enthusiasm, and proved useful to Debussy. He reminded me that I didn't need to reinvent the wheel, nor struggle to come up with new signs and wonders. With good reason, he criticized my excessive penchant for transparency or close-fitting, flesh-colored fabrics that gave the false impression of nudity, leaving too little to the imagination. His words carried the authority of his work. He helped me to step back from myself and take an objective view.

I launched a fashion show at my own expense, which was received like a bad joke, not even causing a real scandal, which would have at least remunerated me in terms of future notoriety. It didn't take place at the Champ de Mars, but in a gallery of modern art. Why not? But what did "modern" mean, anyway? I know now that my work wasn't modern enough, except perhaps the colors. I cursed myself for having compromised, for having paid any heed to the modesty of my models, for having betrayed my own audacity a little more.

I hadn't succeeded in inventing the "polar-opposite suit," which would have entailed the systematic covering of what is usually left undressed—that is, for a body in a public place: face with a mask, hands (sometimes) with gloves, and leaving the rest nude. I mean "leave nude" and not "make nude," which is already one way to turn the world upside down.

I hadn't dared to leave the genitals in plain view. I hadn't even dared—although it was ready, perfected—to dress any of my models in a certain dress that had a vaporous, light-red tinted triangle, against a background of unbleached linen, over the pubic area.

I had, however, adopted a radical approach to the relationship between the usual distance of the fabric from the body, and the manner of its clinging. But was this noticeable enough?

Madame Taillefeu-Ponçard died eight days before my presentation. I found it a terrible stroke of luck at the time, a sentiment that today strikes me as egotistical: what of *her* luck, that day, never mind her advanced age?

Before she passed away, as though she had nothing more important to think about, she had tried to direct some clients my way—four, to be exact—who came to my workshop out of respect for what seemed to them her dying wish. They didn't even offer me their sincere condolences—but this was fair. I wasn't entitled to them. Mostly they expressed a great deal of mistrust, starting out with the conventional phrase:

"Sir, I have nothing to wear."

And soon regretting having said this, since I would respond with:

"Madam, I have very little for you to wear."

"What do you mean?"

"Don't misunderstand me."

I'd undress them with my eye almost to the point of embarrassment, because that was my duty. I couldn't base anything on their spontaneous—that is, uninhibited—desires. It was important, first and foremost, that I trouble them: put them in a state of disequilibrium.

One after the other they bowed out, with the excuse that nudity wasn't quite what they had in mind.

I refused to hire models to allow my customers to see the extent of the scandal I was preparing for them displayed on a neutral party. I wanted to work on my clients themselves, "on your own beast, and right away!" which scandalized them in advance. I refused to let them lend me, as was the practice with their usual dressmakers, their personal mannequins to work with, stuffed with tow-colored hair and lacking lungs that weren't fibrous.

"I need to see you breathe."

"We're not out at the Carreau du Temple market!"

"You breathe everywhere. I need to listen to your chest. Your tailor should see and touch the parts of you that palpitate, should see what your doctor sees. Who knows if I'll need to operate on you, or perform an autopsy? I need to improve the mannequin before I adorn it."

I provoked them. They got on my nerves. I didn't feel like working for them—preferred to work *with* them. Clothing is collaboration. Clothing is a collective affair: the wearer, the conceiver, the contemplator, the dresser and the undresser, the laundress, the ironer . . . and the commentator.

The money I had borrowed for the exposition—or rather the consequences of borrowing it—soon plunged me into the most extreme dependence and small, thankless odd jobs: hands devoted to washing dishes in a trendy seafood restaurant. Hours of black soap, before touching fabric again.

I solicited public subsidies, only to get the response:

"You launch firebrands and ask the most severely burned to finance them! That doesn't make a very good impression."

The word "firebrand" pleased me. Flora Tristan smiled at me from her tomb, and her gaiety mixed in with Madame Taillefeu-Ponçard's. I even thought of my wife who, one day long past, had suffered a kind of stroke of genius: a fever had rooted her to the spot in the fresh air under the moon, her skin all aglow under the nightgown she had torn to shreds. That was the night we made Maurice.

It wasn't only women that inspired me. I thought of my father and his way of coming out of the outhouse in the back of the garden, rain or shine, pajamas at his knees so as not to soil their rear before he reached the bidet. I invented roomy trousers.

Then came the opening of the first grand Colonial Exposition, which, I soon understood, had been arranged by providence especially for my benefit. Crowds of people enthusiastically discovered the novelties of our colonial "outlets," to quote Jules Ferry. *Vive la République exportée!*— because within the République, between its four walls, the very idea of novelty is stifled.

I lived this enthusiasm. I sought this enthusiasm.

The entire universe was there, in microcosm.

I spent all my time in the pavilions, overcome with happiness at the idea that it was possible to go from Cambodia to Natitingou, or from St. Pierre et Miquelon to Bora Bora simply by crossing an alley, in hardly the time it takes to smoke a pipe. The Republic had assembled the most beautiful indigenous peoples of the territories it had now conquered more or less completely. A few slanderous tongues remarked that they were on display "like prize beasts at an agricultural exposition." There was some truth to this, but these exceptional people did me the favor of letting me admire them to my heart's content, and to make all the rough sketches I wanted. I radicalized my colors a little more, having access to foreign materials now, especially the exotic flowers and fruits that were found in abundance there.

I bought a portrait of myself as a Pygmy, done by a photographer who didn't make me stick my face through the hole of a *corps-décor*, but who painted on my skin, taking one hour to work his way from the head to the (penile) artery.

I met Ananwana, a beautiful woman from the Marquesas, who afforded me the most spectacular advances in my art by banishing the last bit of timidity that still restrained me. She was a dancer, but always looked sullen when she danced. Her way of looking sullen paid tribute to the profound difficulty of having to break up the magnificent and limp immobility that was her only defense against her native climate.

One cannot dress properly (in other words, scantily) in a country where it's cold six months out of the year. One can only be *indressed* in Paris about thirty days a year . . . sixty if you're lucky, and that's the final word!

It was October. After *indressing* for me all of September, Ananwana was warming herself by the already-lit stove, and then came the sadness. She was stretched out on a divan showing me her copper-colored back. She was hiding her eyes in her arms, a terrible and heartrending pose. I didn't know she already knew that most of what I'd seen at the Exposition had been embellished.

Ananwana dreamed of returning to the Islands, which was no simple matter. She who knew neither past nor future, who had neither a tomorrow nor memories, had been obliged without warning to come here, to follow this grand deviation of the arrow of time—the most beautiful fleuron of occidental decadence. In order to convince her to come, the colonial administration had lauded her artistic qualities and did its best to smooth over the inevitable asperity of the voyage. But once she arrived safe and sound, not one civil servant had felt the least obligation to make sure she had a pleasant stay in Paris, much less assure that she would be able to make her return journey under conditions comparable to her arrival.

When we met, she was in great need of someone—if not me specifically—in Paris. She danced bewitchingly. I applauded her more than anyone else. I returned each time she was scheduled to dance. I always applauded. How could she not have noticed me? She wanted to know what kind of artist I was myself, and, one thing leading to another, she began living with me. I kept no journal of this beautiful time.

The Exposition ended. I had to arrange Ananwana's departure, though I had no desire for her to leave. But I could see her wasting away.

At the sight of the indifference, or even contempt, of

our government officials, each of whom claimed that it was another's responsibility to deal with the artist's return, I felt deeply ashamed of my civilization. Ananwana stood, waiting, at their offices. No one had asked her to sit down. She was calm and timid, she knew a little French—however butchered—and yet it was *she* who one out of every two of these nincompoops labeled "savage"!

My irritation was of no help to her.

A place opened up, as if by a miracle, on a merchant ship. I put Ananwana on a train that passed the port, wishing her a suitable cabin and a bon voyage, not entirely sure she would have the energy to withstand a month at sea. Would her infinite patience be enough?

In order to commemorate our separation, I made her a dress out of scraps of my own clothes, and made myself an outfit with scraps of her loincloth: clothing in place of the absent being. It makes me sad to wear it.

I never received any news of her. I am very grateful to her.

Ananwana had taught me things in few words. Without saying anything so definitive, she had made me understand without a doubt that I was the savage, that I should face the facts and recognize myself as such; that is to say, return sooner or later to his primitive state, and be among his own kind. She had branded me with the sign of my origins: a little bite mark in the shape of an *S* in the fat of my thigh, reaching just to the blood, which I still have. Ananwana told me that the tooth she'd used to make this mark had been artistically filed for her at puberty, but the artist in question hadn't intended, we suspect, to create something like a typographic stamp of that Latin letter. She didn't want to discuss the symbolism.

"Maybe you could come visit me in the Marquesas."

When the Exposition was over and Ananwana had walked out of my life, I spent several weeks in a torpor. Then I decided to apply for a mission with the Minister of the Colonies. I didn't think I'd have to beg for it for months—as though I wasn't a republican! I was discovering that my Republic was characterized by indecision and stinginess.

"Study fashion in the islands? You must be joking! Don't you know the islanders all go around naked?"

"Precisely!"

If only they'd known just how precisely . . . and besides,

this statement was often, strictly speaking, inaccurate. But all they knew of the overseas territories was what they saw in the catalogs of the Exposition, and that special issue of the *Journal des curieux*.

"You don't seem to understand, Monsieur Paul, that these people represent the past, a past on its way to extinction. If we happen to occupy their lands, it's not because of a miracle, nor is it a result of greed . . . we're only fulfilling a need."

I left them to it. I set out with my pencil, my round chalk, my scissors: tools of precision that, later, I had to trade for a pickaxe or machete more often than not. I worked in Martinique and Panama, went back to France to leave again for Algeria, then French Sudan, because of the Peuhls, who, I told myself, would recognize, to the letter— except for one vowel and that silent *H*—a fellow Paul. I went through the Congo, then to Madagascar. And then to Indochina. From there, Tahiti and the Marquesas. Finally, the Satiety Islands, at which I belatedly obtained my mission, and from where I am now writing my will—as has become increasingly urgent.

But let's examine the stages of my journey one by one.

I left for Martinique as for an imagined Eden. I was very interested in Martinique, but Martinique was only interested in the pencil-pushing I'd admitted to on my résumé. That's what happens when your entire fortune is eaten up by the price of the voyage. I had to do book-keeping, redoing all their sums and verifications, while my sweaty forearms stuck disagreeably to the pages of their account books. This trivial inconvenience added another dreary task (that of un-sticking myself) to an already hope-less and badly paid activity. I still preferred physical work. Moreover, my desire to examine the indigenous people as a part of my investigation of artistic couture was not taken well by the natives. They didn't understand my purpose, and said I was giving them the evil eye, wanting at all costs to see their unhidden loins as having something to do with beauty. I faced a lot of prejudice there, where I'd expected so little of it.

These cousins of the haughty descendants of Toussaint Louverture and Dessalines had already seen too much of we little Whites—those imbecilic and violent planters who had far more consideration for a single stalk of sugarcane than for their slaves.

What was I doing there? I forced myself to try what I had to try, do what I had to do, fighting every inch of the way for the time and the opportunities that were indispensable to my studies. I collected minutes one by one like drops of water in the desert at night. I envied poets and painters who had no need of anyone standing between their canvas or their paper and the outcome they desired for their work. And, periodically, I felt sorry for them for not having the human body—so improvable!—as the final vessel for their work.

In Martinique, people washed their clothes at the same time as their bodies, out in the open for everyone to see, but in water so muddy that one wanted to invent a way to wash the water—a Herculean task—at the same time. The drying (instant for the body, rapid for the cloth), was the best part.

I understood the extent to which repeated washing could soften a personal garment, and that this internalized softness of one's garments is worth more than the simple shell they provide.

I learned from threadbare rags.

I reflected on the stylization of wear and tear.

I undid the stitches in wool sweaters and cheerfully cut

up loincloths. I worked knots like the most conscientious of navy men.

I had the first idea of my "one for two," about which I'll speak at greater length *à propos* of my trip to Cochinchine.

In Martinique, cutting cane yielded nothing. People worked themselves to death at a seasonal job, and when they'd finished, bad rum and illness helped them wait out the time until the next harvest. Everyone dreamed of Panama where they could work digging the canal for what seemed like a dream salary and continuously, for years, without so much as a day of Sunday rest. I set sail for this paradise as soon as I had the money for the voyage: a third-class passenger on the overcrowded deck.

In Colon, I had the luck to be offered a job burying the dead from the dockyards. I soon took notice of the quantity and remarkable regularity of my new arrivals. Malaria and dysentery decimated entire crews, and it would be fair to add work itself to this list of killers, since the explosives they used often blew up for no reason whatsoever and without consideration for those responsible for lighting them. I had to leave. The aesthetic of the shroud had nothing to teach me.

It's impossible to know where my memory has hidden the journeys at sea that brought me back to Le Havre after a largely wasted year. I can't ignore the fact that such years were numerous, monotonous, vegetative. Hands plunged once again into the dishwater of the ship's mess, where would I have found the energy to mediate on aesthetics, to conceive new ideas? Filthy cabins, cockroaches, grease. But on a boat you can't really revolt, lest it be taken for a mutiny and land you, forgotten, in the depths of the hold, if not chucked discreetly overboard (I know what I'm talking about). Still, it didn't suit my character to endure my lot patiently.

I returned to Paris old and burdened with the news of a child dead, my Claire, Claire the Clear, my clarity, who had been dead long enough to be well on the road to decay. My wife's letter was spiteful, certain that I wasn't suffering enough on my own and determined to add to my pain.

In France, I disappeared, hauling my wounds around with me to several provinces where life wasn't too expensive. "In the days when accords served man as bread . . ." I recited La Fontaine, Book IV, Fable 13 to myself, trying to construe my infirmity as a virtue. My home Republic was a desert island, and fairly hostile. I had to look at it differently now. It was autumn. I learned the names of all the seashells of Brittany. In Périgord, the mushrooms. Further north, rosehip and barberry. A good crop and it was paradise. I tasted eggs from all sorts of nests. Who else can boast of having eaten an omelet made from heron's eggs? I made apple preserves and ate persimmons in the leafless trees.

I spent the winter in the country not far from Arles, sharing two miserable rooms, frozen by the mistral, with Vernier, a companion of similar character, except for his fits of madness.

Hector Vernier was a gifted painter who had renounced painting. He had, for two full years, produced some frenzied and inventive work; then, after having exhibited a chamber pot, signing his name and dating it, he turned his tools toward his own body, which decision was of particular interest to me.

He worked in makeup, then particularly in *facial* painting, due to an erroneous reading of the word *facile* in a letter he'd received from his brother. He said he didn't have a penny to buy canvas. It was only too true.

And Vernier skipped essential steps.

As soon as a ray of sun was visible, he exposed himself to it, capriciously masking certain parts of his poor body. The sun tanned him, drawing curves on him in incongruous places, straight lines along the parallels, or crosshatching, or even more curious scrolls. He made, in white, two violin F-holes over his kidneys, simply by sticking bits of cardboard to his body to keep the sun from reaching his skin.

As he was very pale, tanning was perilous. He burned often and suffered without complaint. Soon, red as a lobster in the pot, with the white accents I mentioned, he began to go out on the street completely naked, after having buttered himself with fat, or at other times whitened himself with flour, when there was flour, with plaster, when there was plaster, or with dust, when he couldn't find anything better.

He would go to the museum to undress in front of the visitors. He was often institutionalized.

The police were understanding. But it was often necessary for me to go collect Vernier from them, when they didn't deliver him to me.

One day we had a terrible argument about a body, which made me furious. This body was a woman's. Vernier denied that this body had a woman inside it! I protested that one couldn't speak of human skin like a slough. Certainly he spoke of his own body in similar terms, but that was no excuse. Vernier had wanted to bleed Madeleine in front of me, in order, he said, to leave her intact for me to use afterwards. But as what, a pile of meat? Madeleine who sold her beauty for a living, but who had graciously loaned it to us more than once, reduced to an unconscious heap of leather? Vernier's reasoning became more and more irrational and soon lost all generosity. He made me wonder if the animal—or the man—in him had disappeared entirely. Madeleine flinched before the razor and even bled a little.

"I don't want to see you anymore. You two are too fucked up," Madeleine told me.

I didn't have the courage to say, "It's not me, it's Vernier . . ."

At any rate, Madeleine would never see Vernier again. They locked him up for good. Even his brother didn't come to get him out, except finally to have him brought out feet first after he'd swallowed two metal spoons that he'd carefully sharpened to pierce the stomach. Just before packing my bags, I made some inventive clothing for the neighborhood children's Mardi Gras. This resulted in several cases of bronchitis.

I hadn't given up on obtaining my famous scientific mission to the primitive environment of the tropics from the Minister of the Colonies and the Colonial Administration. I drew up plan after plan, applying to ad hoc commissions, careful not to talk to them about my rags. I only wanted to go in order to study primitive religions, which we needed to know more about in order to impose our own, developed, sugarcoated, syncretistic religion on the natives (submitted to the clergy); or else in order to curb the activities of our overzealous missionaries (submitted to the anticlericals). Moreover, I outlined studies of the subsoil of Madagascar and its presumed riches, as well as of local customs: all information that would permit the colonists to fuck the inoffensive indigenous peoples up the ass all the more easily. Nobody said so in so many words, of course, but that's what it boiled down to. I wanted to trick the Administration into giving me what I wanted by pretending to share its presumed intentions. Was I convincing enough, given how unconvinced I was? But I wanted to achieve my own ends.

The Arles post office often saw me come in laden with my official love letters, and likewise saw me reappear a little later to collect the refusals in the *poste restante* bags.

"They only send thieves and scoundrels out there," an old colonial who had been in Sudan told me. "Certainly not men of conviction, especially if they're Republicans. Make some shady intentions known, discreetly, and everything will work out. As long as you're not the scion of a high-class family, with two or three years of military school behind you, and a specialization in engineering . . . though, come to think of it, none of that necessarily excludes you from being a scoundrel."

I waited impatiently, utterly enraged, until the day when I finally received orders to present myself to the Peuhl, after traversing the desert. Had my luck finally changed?

Paul went to the Peuhl by boat, on camelback, on foot. He crossed the small, fertile band of Algeria, then the vast desert. He shivered at night and panted by day. He tanned his hide and learned to take his time. At the end of the road, he discovered the African body, with plenty of vestimentary solutions that he had already, naively, reinvented. This world, however, was secret. The males didn't wear clothes until after circumcision. Before, they went naked. After being married, Muslim Peuhl women were entirely hidden in veils, from their heads to the tips of their toes and fingers, before throwing themselves into procreation, and other small tasks. Paul also discovered that colonial society had different worries from his own: missionaries imposing "modest" dress, entrepreneurs mad about efficiency. It was a shame. The encounter between White and Black was about to be botched, though this mistake wasn't necessarily fatal. The Black was curious about the White, the White about the Black. Some French officers, whose legal wives were back in the mother country, had black co-spouses; thus, some black women had white (co-?)spouses. Some men officially recognized their mixed-race children. Violence, when it occurred, was shared. I saw some black children, beaming, drag the body of a bandit as black as themselves to the communal grave, after he had been summarily executed by the grown-ups. Though they wouldn't have been able to do as much with a white. I saw colonists' children authorized by their parents to make a black thief jump onto dynamite (they certainly wouldn't have done as much to a white). Many of the personal relationships had a real strength to them, but this was ruined by the colonial hierarchies, and the concept of work:

"They don't know how to work, and they don't want to."

"Well then, don't ask them to! Listen to them sing, pay them to dance for a bit of millet, *dolo* (millet beer), or *fonio*. And end the famines that way, if you're so industrious!"

"You haven't been in Sudan for long, have you? You talk like you're right off the boat!"

I cursed the skin colors that instantly announced the *de facto* hierarchy of the colony. Whites had their uniforms and their decoration. Blacks had scarifications.

I invented outfits that were conceived as frames for the scars of the wearer. My Cesarean dress caused a scandal. The woman who wanted to wear it was rejected by her people and exiled to the bush. But perhaps the real reason for her exile was that her son had died at an early age. My wooden bell costume exhausted dancers. My prototypes for unfastened fasteners and closed openings unnerved the impatient.

I wanted to create rituals of dressing and undressing, like there are in so many societies at the time of marriage. But I ran up against the paradox of ritual's own disapproval for invention, precisely because invention is itself a form of ritual.

I consoled myself with the landscape made of long, bare lines. While walking in the brush, I benefited from the slowness I had learned.

I was not consoled by the famine, however, when it raged that year, though I learned then the extent to which clothing can be what makes one look healthy, its color being so close to that of fine foods; learning too that the absence of food can become so visible in one's complexion that it makes inferior cloth look gray. Jam, food for the body; *boubou*, food for the soul. But one doesn't eat with one's eyes, contrary to the old saying.

I had rediscovered, in Niger, the savage nonchalance that Ananwana had initially introduced me to. Here, she was called Maïrama. She drew patterns for me in the sand so I could make innovative fabrics using them. The natural capacities of her pose, and above all the art of transformation, rising from the mat ... the least bit of cloth making up thirty-two possible forms of evening dress, according to the diverse ways of folding or knotting ... the marvelous knots ... I only had to open my eyes and observe this square of cloth on the body, its way of enveloping, of hugging, of releasing . . . hiding its corners by tucking them under the breasts or underarms. For her in particular, I looked for a fabric redder and sweeter than rose-hip marmalade.

A wool scarf, the veils of Indian sculpture, the *perizonium* of Christ, the little angel in swaddling clothes on Rhenish altarpieces—these all blended together in my memory.

Again, I ask myself why that wasn't enough.

Maïrama, when she talked about her ancestors, always employed a temporal paradox, "My future ancestor, my future grandmother," which coincided logically, however, with the moment in time in which she was situating the person. In her way of thinking, when her grandmother was a child, she could only be Maïrama's future grandmother, and then a future dearly departed; that is to say, a living dead woman . . . time, with its three facets, was already lost to her.

Maïrama had moments of great sadness, during which I would see nothing but her back on the mat. Backs of women are consumed by anguish, submerged, balled up in their anguish because they do everything more completely than men—these women whom we must love to the point of anguish. It's difficult. When we treat them like nuisances, we commit a judicious error. Women are always unhappier than us. Are they also happier if need be? Why wasn't I born a she?

Maïrama didn't always understand why I was so interested in her clothing, or even in her body. She didn't see the sense in it. The sense of sight was not, for her, the dominant sense, particularly in the domain of love. Smell and touch—senses that prefer the night, that demand the darkest dark—were, for her, the best grounding for our embraces, under the noisy flights of bats, fat like the pheasants at home.

I learned something from this experience of darkness. It was necessary to create, in clothing, a sort of optical illusion with the material: am I looking at the skin yet, or is it just another layer of very soft silk? And, too: how could a perfume be made intrinsic to a fabric and yet lead directly into another? How could one nest scents together like colors in the depths of certain enamels?

I spent nights of exaltation conceiving my clothing-universe, conceiving a kind of global wardrobe that would put an end to hot and cold, nudity and covering, beauty and ugliness—leaving simply what happens, all that happens, nothing but what can happen, all that we don't even know has a possibility of happening.

These were visionary intuitions.

In reality, though . . . if I put it all on the table . . . Well, I hadn't invented anything. I was working in a field where nothing is ever really invented, because there's nothing left to invent; because even the most vibrant clothing is nothing when it's hanging in a closet, but everything when it's being put on, worn, and then taken off. Everything in this industry is, quite simply, received, passed along—one is nothing more than a conduit. I'm not against being a passageway, mind you: this passing along is the purest, truest quality of the art, and never pompous; even if the most striking exceptions, those innovators who seem to halt the movement of this passage with their idiosyncrasies, appear to contradict this theory. So we say and hear it said that there are only one or two real artists per century and per continent that really matter. The problem with these idiotic lists of award winners is that all the other artists— the ones who row boats and serve the soup for the award winners—work just as hard, and sell their hard work or offer it graciously for nothing more than a few, supposedly valuable, government bonds. But there are no guarantees—sure things are always going sour—and the truth is that the originators of the most enlightened philosophies are never remunerated with anything more than an embarrassed and condescending acquiescence. Society's perpetual aim is to forget that anything ever happened.

But why the hell did I have want to be somebody anyway? Enough! If I succeeded, what place would my teacher, Madame Taillefeu-Ponçard, earn in history? What recognition would Ananwana and Maïrama receive? Do people know the name of a single medieval or Babylonian sculptor? Let it be enough that I create, and may I never go down in history as an isolated phenomenon! Well, old boy, the answer is simple: form a group! Establish yourself from within a group photo! But it was no use. I hadn't inspired any followers.

I was ill in the Congo. All I remember is my bouts of delirium, and that I frightened the nuns, who saved my life anyway.

In Madagascar I took in the scenery as fast as I could. It wasn't like the desert of Niger, but a liberating mix of greens and reds, so different from our too-subtle European palate . . . with vast distances undulating so vibrantly, it seemed you could reach out and touch them.

In Madagascar, I paid no attention to the official costume, because there was a sharp and youthful governor running the place, utopist and kind, who everyone thought was an imbecile. This is something I need to describe in detail.

I met Governor Le Balatonier on the boat, between Port Elizabeth and Tamatave, when he was on his way to assume his post. Since he was as new as I was to the big island, we were reduced to recounting our previous experiences in order to make conversation. This brought us closer together. He had been to Ubangi and Gabon. His goal with regard to his post was to find a way to avoid looking too colonial without actually going native.

"They think we're superior men, to a certain extent. Fine. It's not a serious problem, but to set them straight would be suicide. And then there are the soldiers . . . I don't have a problem with them, and I don't want to take anything away from them. But the hard and fast republican layman must also have his costume, which can hardly be that of the Mayor of Saint-Nom-la-Bretèche, if you see what I'm saying . . . Look at the Saint-Simonians: there are some boys who've put some real thought into their clothing. And we other Masons . . . While we're waiting, let's get to know our hosts!"

I tried to learn a little Malagasy from a local book meant for beginning students of French. "Lesson One: 1. *Manao ahoana ny rano? 2. Maloto ny rano. 3. Maloto be ny rano? 4. Maloto ve ny rano? 5. Eny, maloto ny rano. 6. Maloto be ve ny rano? 7. Eny, maloto be ny rano . . .*

"1. How is the water? 2. The water is dirty. 3. The water is very dirty. 4. Is the water dirty? 5. Yes, the water is dirty. 6. Is the water very dirty? 7. Yes, the water is very dirty. 8. The water is not dirty. 9. The water is not very dirty. 10. Isn't the water dirty? 11. No, the water isn't dirty. 12. Isn't the water very dirty? 13. No, the water is not very dirty. 14. How is the house? 15. The house is clean . . ."

Ugh. I'm not making this up. I did not learn Malagasy.

I began to work by examining Governor Le Balatonier's paunch, which I didn't really know how to work with—I should say, after I'd weighed it in my mind and decided that it wasn't going to melt away.

I told myself I'd have to address his back, or at least start there, so I turned his coat around.

57

Le Balatonier's dress coat, as soon as I'd inverted the orientation, came together pretty much by itself. I could easily allow it a certain Parisian rigor without feeling obliged to deal with the primarily functional openings, except for certain trompe l'oeil effects: false buttons, pockets, lapels, at the borders of which I allowed myself vents that were almost violent: parentheses, zebra stripes, dry slits in the fabric that were supposed to evoke machete cuts in white skin, supposed to represent the blood of a calf or fowl refusing to be shed, as it should in an invulnerable body. My work required careful research (as patient as Gutenberg taking his time making an ink that was neither too fluid nor not fluid enough) to find a discrete way to starch the lips of these slits. I used kaolin.

Le Balatonier was such a perfectly pleasant person to do business with that his initial reaction to my creation didn't give me any forewarning of the public catastrophe to come. Between the two of us all he said was that he thought my ego was swollen, while in public he exhausted all his energy in talking up the good points of my creation—points that his entourage, guffawing with laughter, did not see; nor indeed did the major designers of Tananarive, who were furious about his get-up . . . that is to say, about having to bow to it. Le Balatonier was my only customer.

People pointed at me even while turning their backs on me. I cursed my country. I shat on it without discretion. And, in the same vein, I cursed our host country for submitting to it, because they wanted to be conquered again.

When I told whoever would listen about my hatred of my country and my culture, even my culture and my country's worst enemies showed a violent incomprehension: How is this possible? What about your parents? Where are your children? You don't know where your children are? Your children hate you? You say your father was an imbecile and your mother was a fool? What do your kids say about you? How is all this possible? Don't you know you can never have too many spirits watching over you? You have to keep a tally of them, one by one, on the broad surface of your heart. And you have to go back to see them every year, go back for a long visit, turn them over in their holes in the ground. Don't you have any respect for your elders? Why don't your children come to see you? Don't you want to touch your wife anymore? Here, it's our women who don't want to touch you. Take our advice. Be on your way. Flee the camp. Don't worry about us.

Faces furious, they raised their fists, ready to hit me. What do you want? A Peuhl looks red to a Mossi, and if you listen to him, a northern Mossi is less black than a southern Mossi. The Merina and the Mahafale hate each other. And the Northern Mahafale and the Southern Mahafale kill each other. Sell wooden stakes and chevaux-de-frise, and then you'll be in business! We've corrupted you.

Where was the savage? The savage . . . the savage I was looking for didn't soak his hands in blood and show them to the throng, didn't eat raw kidneys or livers. Nor was he some sickly sweet, passionless savage, even more of a half-wit than Montaigne's or Jean-Jacques's. I realized, finally, that my civilized civilization was unlikely to be willing to consume a bit of savagery like a vitamin or a periodic purgative, designed to reveal all the supposedly provisional immorality of our way of life. I fell off my high horse. Improving the Republic was impossible. One had to reject it, pure and simple. It was for this reason that some poets, with whom I felt in tune, emphasized the negative energy inside of beauty. It was for this reason that some planted bombs in Paris—real, metal bombs, built with timers to allow the culprit time to flee. I couldn't do it anymore. I couldn't keep living there, in Tananarive, couldn't continue making my infernal machines.

I arrived in Indochina without first going back to the mother country. There were a lot of people there—that was the first thing I noticed. Men and women of all ages walking right on top of each other without any apparent emotion. The landscape could be empty one second and filled with people the next. Then, everything would disappear again. It was opaque. Their bodies were distracted. I couldn't grasp the details and circumstances of their probable human anguish as I could with others. I knew right away that it wasn't the place for me.

I may have been a faltering artist, but I tried nevertheless to get a few original and pertinent ideas across. The only real innovation I discovered was based on cell division, meiosis or mitosis: a couple could buy one garment and, after my intervention, both of them would be able to clothe themselves with it, clothe themselves partially, since the climate allowed it. The Indochinese frame didn't possess the massive character that the African body often had.

My designs can still be found in certain old Saigon *Nouvelles Galeries* catalogs; that is, if that kind of retailer keeps archives.

I earned a little money, but I didn't get a swelled head about it. After a number of days, among the most arduous I'd ever known, I began to dream of moving again. "It seems to me that I should always be happier elsewhere than where I happen to be,"[‡] said dear Baudelaire. I frequented Saigon's rowdiest bars, where other dromomaniacs recounted the tales of their past journeys with a richness of detail equaled only by the eloquence of their rhetoric. From early on, anyone who lived starting their life over again every fourth morning recognized a sister soul in me—the sister soul that loosens the tongue (if in fact souls have tongues)—always dreaming of the port's coming alive, the steamer *Armand-Béhic* arriving from Marseilles, docking for two days before casting off for Noumea . . .

"The more I look at you, the more I see you in the Satiety Islands," said a man with a wooden leg, which, I swear, I saw trembling with emotion.

The leg informed me that I still hadn't seen the real savage, the Polynesian, he who only swears by the "poly-"!

Long live the poly-, glory be to the name of the poly-! Far from any spirit of unity, far from the monody! Let all sides of the body pass at once, in all directions, not one by one, as Hugo, Hector Vernier's brother, would say. The spit impales the rooster and comes out his crowing mouth, and there he is stuck on top of the belfry tower, at the mercy of the four winds. Death to the civilized Paul with his Republic's gluttonous capital, never satiated! The franc is, frankly, useless. I plunge into the abyss. To fish, to dive towards fish, to gather the fruit of the breadfruit tree, fe'i bananas, pearls. Even war is healthy there. Welcome, paul-the-poly, in lowercase, one among so many other poly-s, and so "poly-" himself that it would be more appropriate to use the plural, to say "poly- *themselves*"; turned any which way, like a domino, embracing anything and everything that happens, under the sun, barely dressed, unsexed entirely or else having become nothing *but* sex, impolite, violent, tender. I slipped into the skin of this archipelago, having abandoned any pride I might have had in my origins. Wholesome hay, shit underneath. Fashion isn't pure, soap isn't pure, pure water isn't pure, intentions aren't pure, and let's not even mention the air . . . even origins aren't pure, and God is pure pustulation. Long live Ananwana, with whom I would surely be reunited. Let's drink some more—it's impure. I am the enemy of God, just as I'm the enemy of the Republic and all that is honest. I'm an activist for public uselessness.

Much as I'd so recently organized Ananwana's departure, my own departure was also organized by others, particularly the French mercantile houses of Indochina, which preferred to see me far away so that they could tone down my designs to suit their own tastes. But I had become indifferent to that. Docilely at first, and then enthusiastically, I set out for the Satiety Islands.

Before Satiety, I stopped in at the Marquesas, where I didn't find the slightest trace of Ananwana, despite an ardent search.

What I did see there was cruel.

I had painted a picture in my imagination of resplendent landscapes with soft shadows and mud and thatch houses. In reality there were only poorly finished dwellings of exposed brick and corrugated iron, stupidly conducting heat without combating the humidity. These mediocre dwellings slouched on treeless strips of land: nothing but bare stumps were left and nothing had been planted to replace what had been cut down. It was sad and arid, like a police station in the Hoggar.

When I met the king at a reception, he no longer practiced the beautiful rituals of which I had heard lovely voices speak, or had read about in books. He had sold his land to France and his power to the governor. He lived for alcohol. His eyes were eloquent. His borrowed clothes were poorly buttoned. They were made up of various secondhand sacerdotal vestments that the Church had offered him. He begged drinks off visitors. Even I, who was against the bishop and in favor of alcohol, could only see how well they'd scourged this man in tandem—the same ravages I myself could look forward to, no doubt, if I continued to drink and howl against the skullcaps. The king was flaccid. He made no attempt to hold a conversation lasting longer than one sentence. People told me that his family had been wiped out—one of his sons, as syphilitic as I was, had drunk himself to death. He'd sold his island for a variety of booze—champagne, beer, absinthe, whiskey, local rum, cheap red wine, and Grand Marnier—all mixed together into an immense cocktail, defying all the rules of drinking, and kept in a watertight canoe from which the lush would drink, regularly, bent over it like an animal by a trough.

The queen, who still maintained a fairly dignified bearing, walked around like a ghost. She was pale and hardened by the decadence around her, but had given up on trying to vanquish it, and then even putting up any resistance to it. She had a collection of five thousand pairs of shoes, from all provenances, often secondhand, that fit her poorly. She spent her days trying them on and negotiating their repair with her three utterly unskilled cobblers. I had the privilege of laying eyes on this collection: a stinking mountain of shoes, waiting to be dealt with and smelling of the deaths of their former owners. I didn't say a word, but made myself as small as I could, afraid the queen would ask me to work for her, a job that the French Administration would certainly have forced me to accept.

Because I was on assignment, people thought I was like all the other French. The officials in civil service wanted me for their own; the colonels likewise. What luck! I was forced to choose between crap and shit. Colonels and civil servants are always in covert conflict, attacking each other with denunciations and anonymous letters. The colonels didn't see the point of the administrators, whose only desire was to limit their own capacity for resourcefulness. A governor who mingled in order to seem enlightened could count his days. Soldiers arbitrated between the administration and the natives, all the while maintaining the divisions that assured their rule. The French mercantile houses of Oceania were able to sell potatoes from Bauce and Picardie by sabotaging the local production of yams, wild bananas, breadfruit, and the sweet potato, which remained the primary food of the savages. The tiniest square of cloth came from Roubaix, all metal objects from Longwy, and cigarettes from the black market. Smoking pandanus leaf was forbidden! And life was more expensive here than in Paris. It was impossible to find even the smallest object that had actually been constructed locally—nothing made of sequoia wood or bamboo with its natural sheen. The local weavers had lost the touch. They tropicalized themselves by ceasing to work, consecrating themselves to dominos or cards—bridge for the bourgeoisie. When they weren't involved in some kind of lawsuit, the people of this beautiful society danced in huge, unified crowds, pulsating, under the governor's authority. Chinese infiltrators, Brits, and Indians tenaciously ate up the market shares and small shops. More than one of them—rarely a Brit, though—found a knife between his shoulder blades. The Catholics and the Protestants competed for conversions, same as the Muslims and Catholics in Lower Niger. It was monotheist Europe with its religious wars all over again.

Did anyone remember anything about the Marquesan traditions, or had they too been forgotten, like the traditions of the Maori who'd preceded them? Children worshipped the Virgin Mary, and old people worshipped Benedictine. The missionaries didn't bother to correct their converts when, in chorus, they prayed to the Virgin Maori.

People had spoken to me of the loose morals on the Islands, but when I was told not to miss the "meat market," it still took me a moment to realize they were talking about the red-light district. I became a pillar of that particular society.

The population was melting right before my eyes; the mortality rate was horrifying: miscarriages, syphilis. And Western taxation up until the moment of burial.

I felt like ripping off the French clothing I saw on shoulders everywhere—whether they were French shoulders or not.

July 14th took the cake. Bastille Day in the Marquesas! I heard the men's choir of the villages of Anjou, then the accordion and the guitar. The smallest tom-tom, the tiniest local flute, had all been burned in the fire of joy that the Marquesans themselves—wearing second- or third-hand khakis—fed with logs. Raffles inspired dreams of winning a sewing machine in the locals, while in my own creations I was striving toward wraps without additions: natural hems, edging without loops, buttonholes, or buttons: clothes were the continuity of the body, according to Madame Taillefeu-Ponçard's continuity of thought. Parisian straps, unfortunately, infuriated me. "La Marseillaise" was fervently butchered by jovial voices.

"You have to take it further," the wooden leg in Saigon had said. It was right.

Of course I wanted to take it further . . . but not without a certain anxiety—that the Earth was, in fact, round, as is generally accepted, and that at the end of the road I'd just end up back within sight of the Port of Marseilles.

I procured a rudimentary boat and the services of an impassive fisherman who kept his eyes on the prow of his boat.

I left the Marquesas at five o'clock.

Days and days on the water and under the sun . . . the *floc-floc* of the oars and the uselessness of the sail . . . I expected to turn into charcoal, crammed with raw fish and lacking fresh water.

One week later, I reached the Satiety Islands at last.

I had never known such clarity, such certainty about the future: I would never leave the Satieties, no matter what surprises awaited me there.

The landscape had something edge-of-the-worldly about it, like a big backdrop that all the sailors in the sea could come to lean against. From time to time a cloud, the least menacing cloud possible, would catch on the peak of a mountain. And none of the natives of those immutable islands would puff their cheeks and blow towards the sky to try to push it away. Had time somehow stopped on this island?

For a few days, it almost seemed that way.

And then I began to perceive the insidious decline of everything we had touched since the captains of the first ships arrived.

Alcohol was still an issue, albeit more covert.

The degradation had not progressed as far as in the

Marquesas or Papeete. It was Papeete thirty years earlier. Already the policemen could be heard proclaiming, "No nude bathing!"

"No nudity even at home!" declared the clergy. "Greet me when I pass, and think of your soul, of salvation!" I don't even want to know what the Church was doing to the young girls it claimed to protect.

The fruit was not always at the peak of ripeness, the women were not eternally beautiful. Corruption did exist.

It wasn't all I had expected, but some charming traces of that idea still remained. When, far away, I dreamed of this haven, I'd dreamed of an immense scenic garment, one loincloth for the entire population, the color of sky and the local flora: a garment that would clothe two hundred individuals at once, individuals who were capable of devoting themselves to their jobs, neither becoming slaves nor separating themselves from their community. Yes, there was still a little remaining here of the old savagery, from before the time of the present-day savages, who didn't bare their teeth or show their claws.

Like a ray of sun before a fateful tempest, I found an attentive ear in a cultured traveler named Monsieur Jabert, who had heard of my theories on fashion and understood perfectly what I was trying to accomplish (even if what little demonic reputation I had was already slightly dated and losing its bite). He offered to sell my progressive designs for me, in the London-Paris-Berlin triangle, to the cabaret set, the strip-club set, and the frequenters of *café-concerts*—designs they would certainly enjoy, on both sides of the footlights. His compliments did the trick. I allowed myself to be convinced.

I got back to work, shaking off the ghosts of Manet, Hector Vernier, and Mme Taillefeu-Ponçard, trying to recapture Ananwana's perfumes, Maïrama's cures, and Madeleine's nervousness. I completed—successfully, I think—designs that gave the shoulders a dominant position and lengthened the sides of the body, showing an uninterrupted strip of skin from the ankle all the way to the underarm, while the front and back were to be covered in supple pleats, knotted at the crotch.

M. Jabert only asked me for prototypes, offering to have them duplicated in his workshops on the outskirts of London. But, as I might have known, the Satiety colonial government threw a wrench in the works.

All authority was concentrated in the person of the Islands' single policeman, the prototypical pig who had abandoned all self-control. He used force to assure that he himself held all the local positions of power: cop, court clerk, bailiff, attorney, judge, advocate, notary, customs official, harbormaster, postmaster, tax collector . . . with so much power, it was a miracle he abused it so little.

When I found out that the chief of police and some other low-ranking official was keeping a close watch on our exports and wanted to delay until the next boat—in other words, by a good two months, at best—my heart skipped a beat (accelerated by the alcohol that had diluted my blood) . . . in return, I beat it over to the chief's place and proceeded to beat him senseless, which turned out to be the worst thing I could have done, as he and Monsieur Jabert had already agreed on baksheesh and settled the issue.

I found myself in jail, exhausted, devoid of any desire for anything. Monsieur Jabert had left with my designs. The percentage that came back to me was reasonable. When—with all the speed of the next boat arriving from civilization—the money finally reached me, it was just enough to guarantee my freedom.

Upon my release, I was buttonholed by a native with a strange face. He was dressed in a vast toga that enveloped him completely. He signaled for me to follow him. His gait was hindered by the folds of his toga, to which he was obviously not accustomed. Moreover, as soon as he had disappeared into the leafy vegetation with me at his heels, he dropped the garment.

Underneath, he was not naked. He was skinned. But this sight, though unexpected, didn't faze me.

I had heard about the Sect of the Flayed, but had never completely believed that such a thing existed. The man's appearance erased any doubts I might have had. From his chest to the tips of his toes, he had no skin. What was already startling on his limbs—the petrified appearance of the muscles—became downright frightening where his viscera were visible, protected from the external environment by nothing more than a sort of vermiculated pleura, a bit like the flat sausage of my old country, which we called *crépinette*. He regarded me without violence, without sadness. He did not provoke me. I could see the bottom of his bright red lungs inflating and deflating, a normal respiratory rhythm. His long member looked like a chicken's neck. His muscle tissue had been cured. I would later be able to attest to the viability of this technique. When he had understood that I wasn't going to run, and that my repulsion was considerably surpassed by my curiosity, he turned his back towards me and continued the journey. I studied the muscles of his thighs in action. And soon, we came to a cave.

In the cave there was the smell of burning, an impression of hygiene. The men and women who lived and grew up here were all flayed to different degrees. There was a perceptible hierarchy in the weave of the muscle tissue in the face of a woman whose eyes no longer closed. In a corner of the cave, a man was removing the skin of a newborn's hand. A patient who was waiting, seated on a rock, pointed happily to the skin on his abdomen, a little like a client at the hairdresser's would, making me understand that an hour later he'd be free of it.

At no time did I feel in danger. No one made me feel that they had their eyes on my hide. Obviously, the only way to explain the invitation that I'd received was to suppose that the Sect of the Flayed saw me as a connoisseur, recognized me as a kindred spirit, with whom it would be advisable to hold a symposium. Raising my eyes toward the naturally domed ceiling of the grotto, I noticed the equivalent of what one sees in the Dry Room of a Western mine up in its heights: the miners' clothes hung out to dry where the heat collects . . . except here, in the cave, they were human skins, complete envelopes pieced together like dreams.

In a sort of game that I'd half been expecting, they motioned for me to pull down their creations for a closer look. Was I supposed to choose one? I indicated one that was female on its left side and male on its right, but no one made a move to put it on, and it didn't seem that anyone expected me to do so, either. Was the idea to contemplate, perhaps to admire, the technique, the aesthetic? Yes, certainly: to muse over it.

I stayed with the Flayed for several days, enough time to examine all the skins. No one asked anything of me. They brought me food and drink—fruit juices and clear water, boiled vegetables.

Finally, I wasn't able to muster the energy to remain there, to remain in that state of inertia. I was a man whose time was about to run out. I returned to the village, with its small port, its small passions, its small prison. With its petty hopes and pathetic memories.

I knew I'd never be a savage. I knew it now more surely than ever—now that I'd spent a few days truly being one: loving the present, without nostalgia or hope, with no thought of what might lay upstream or down—the present, at the only price I could imagine for it—as I remember it, as I relive it—at once new and antediluvian—in a flash. This is my testament.

I made more patterns for M. Jabert.

I began to earn a regular living, but that didn't interest me. There's nothing there to interest me. Besides, I spend everything long before I get paid.

I found myself on the street, penniless and sick—and the local doctor is a friend of our one policeman.

I slept for days under the influence of laudanum, dreaming that I was watching Ananwana, or being watched by her.

I think of she who is coming back. She who is coming back is thinking of me.

Maïrama dreams she's a gecko. The gecko dreams he's Maïrama.

Pauline and Madeleine take turns watching the children.

The trees in the wind bend until they brush the soil.

Yesterday I discovered what a cyclone really is. Today, the torrents of rain and the flooding.

I still draw a little, though less and less: I don't have the eyes for it anymore. Writing is no longer possible, but I can still dictate.

I sew blindly. A woman sits with me to cut the thread.

I'm going to stop dictating shortly; I feel a fit coming on. I don't know if it's day or night. I don't want any more laudanum.

I don't even want my bandages changed anymore.

ADDITIONS

Since the documents that make up this novel (with a certain amount of material borrowed, necessarily, from Paul
Gauguin's biographers, particularly Bengt Danielsson, *Gauguin in the South Seas*, 1966) weren't found in a crawlspace
under the stairs, under a loose stone in the vault of the
Chateau de Mormoiron, or even in the calfskin cover of an
old missal, there's no reason another attempt shouldn't now
be made, after its false-real conclusion. Its story not having
been heard recounted by an abhorred companion while
sitting around a fire; not having found it copied out, under
the dictation of a translator-captain, by an officer under
siege at Saragossa; and not knowing upon whom I might
perhaps be bestowing some amount of pleasure by printing
the pages that compose this text and making them public,
I could hardly consider this novel complete without giving
the reader a couple of additional accounts, every bit as fic-
tional as the story that preceded them; additions that were

not found in Dr. Ralph's pockets when he died at Minden, in the Year of Our Lord 1759.

For the sake of the different perspective they add to the body of existing evidence, their presence here is essential.

INTERVIEW ON THE SUBJECT OF CLOTHING
(EXCERPTS), PUBLISHED IN 1899 IN THE
JOURNAL DES DÉBATS.

Q: Clothing?

A: You're asking me what clothing is. What do you hope to learn? Clothing is anything one wants it to be, obviously. Everything we want and everything we see. If you insist that I answer this question, I would like to tell you what clothing is *to me.*

Q: Please.

A: But will you understand? We'll see. There is no clothing except the clothing you traverse.

Q: What do you mean by that?

A: Just as I thought . . . It's simple: in clothing, the world passes you by as never before. So, you *become* its passage without being, despite this, transported oneself. That's real presence. Your troubles are as inoffensive as a hornet in a hurricane. You are neither dressed nor naked; it's the story of the fisherman's net. You see?

Q: I don't. Please elaborate.

A: It's a challenge. You wrap yourself in fishing net, like a toga. Then you attach the carcass of a lobster next to a cork. When I say that the world should pass by you, well, obviously, you're part of the world as well, you're a piece of it. Thus, your clothes should be traversed by the present moment, by the current season, by the weather of the moment, by roving hands, by your own bones, holding your skin taut, by . . .

Q: Calm down . . .

A: I will not calm down! Go on! Do as I say! Dress yourself in glass or a cocoon of silk. Start by undressing from head to toe. Part your hair—all your hair. Get to know all the hairy parts of man's body: his head, his eyebrows, his eyelashes, his upper lip, his chin, his armpits, his lower belly, his asshole! What, does that offend you? Fine, then! Fine! We can both just shut up!

Thus concludes, abruptly, our conversation with the famous Paul, the "unsuitable suit maker," or the "un-suit maker," as he's known all over the fashion districts of Paris. A lot of eructation for nothing, I must say. But we have to see it for what it is: an eccentric exception, and one that will perhaps serve as a reservoir of ideas for some future designer, fresh out of school.

. . . When Paul arrived on the Satiety Islands, his behavior seemed most violent. He was looking for a piece of ass, that's all; his supposed chastity was a lie. He wanted to stay naked all the time and live in a permanent state of arousal. He was vicious with everyone and it didn't do him the least bit of good. He harbored an extreme, unreasonable hatred for the Chinese, for example. I was the only one who understood his distress. I was retired, a former customs official spending my retirement in Satiety. He was an unfortunate friend. He played an accordion with the bellows split open, and he composed music for this hole. That's honestly what he said. He pursued women, but always scared them away. When he had "shackled" one, as he put it, he celebrated for two days and then became bored. He was violent, as I said: he even drank violently. He loved my almond brittle, a specialty of mine, a hard paste of chopped almonds and cashews, which sucked up all the alcohol in his body. It was harder and harder for him to . . . women wanted nothing more to do with him. He had a lover at the end of his life, a Satiety native whose only dream was to be a cowboy in the Wild West. That put Paul in a real mood. They fought. Paul could be both stingy and generous; he ended up owing me a great deal. He made very curious outfits for me, which I wore so as not to insult him, but I didn't keep them. There are no photographs left of them; he didn't much care for photography, to say the least. In fact, he had a veritable phobia of it. His last moments? You'll have to talk to the old Pohao, the medicine man. He was the one to bite his head, as they do here, to make sure he was really dead.

Translator's Notes

p. 10   This phrase is an allusion to Jean-Paul Sartre's work, *The Family Idiot.* The author modifies Sartre's phrase, *"Que peut-on savoir de l'homme aujourd'hui?"* ("What, at this point in time, can one know about a man?" in Carol Cosman's translation) by changing the verb *"savoir"* (to know) to *"inventer"* (to invent).

p. 62   From Baudelaire's poem "Anywhere out of this World," translated by Arthur Symons.

SELECTED DALKEY ARCHIVE PAPERBACKS

FOR A FULL LIST OF PUBLICATIONS, VISIT:
www.dalkeyarchive.com

SELECTED DALKEY ARCHIVE PAPERBACKS

FOR A FULL LIST OF PUBLICATIONS, VISIT:
www.dalkeyarchive.com